Grandma's Promise

Grandma's Promise

Story by Elaine Moore · Pictures by Elise Primavera

Lothrop, Lee & Shepard Books   New York

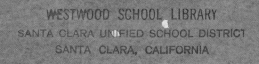

First Edition 1 2 3 4 5 6 7 8 9 10

Library of Congress Cataloging in Publication Data
Moore, Elaine.   Grandma's promise.
Summary: Kim spends a week after Christmas with her grandmother and enjoys every minute—sleeping by the wood stove, ice
skating on the pond, and feeding the birds.   [1. Grandmothers—Fiction]   I. Primavera, Elise, ill.   II. Title.
PZ7.M7832Gs 1988   [E]   86-33762
ISBN 0-688-06740-9 ISBN 0-688-06741-7 (lib. bdg.)

Printed in Singapore.

To Mike
E. M.

To my grandmother, Margaret Miller
E. P.

I ALWAYS LIKE CHRISTMAS, but this year I like after Christmas, too. I am going to spend a week with Grandma.

At the airport, I jump and shout when I see Grandma. She hurries through the crowd to meet me. "Kim," she exclaims, "you've grown!"

"Not you, Grandma," I say. "You always look the same."

Grandma laughs and I laugh too. Then we climb into her truck and drive the bumpy road to Grandma's house.

Once we're inside, I rush to touch everything I have touched before. I look to see if anything is new. My bed is different; it is piled high with quilts. I have never been to Grandma's in the winter before.

At bedtime Grandma tells me a story about a little girl named Kim. I feel cozy and warm under my quilts. Listening to Grandma's soft voice, I wish the story would never end.

The next morning a bright light streams into my room. My window is a white peephole. I throw back the covers and scramble to look out.

"Snow!" I yell. "Grandma, it snowed!"

When Grandma comes upstairs, she has news too. Because of the storm, we have no electricity.

"Don't worry," she says. "We have the lantern for light and the wood stove for heat. We have everything we need, but it's cold up here. Let's go down to the kitchen where it's warm."

Downstairs, Grandma says, "Would you fetch me a jar of our peaches?"

On Grandma's pantry shelves are rows of shimmering glass jars. I see strawberry jam, string beans, tomatoes, and the peaches I helped Grandma pick last summer.

Grandma drops chunks of fruit into oatmeal bubbling on the wood stove. Soon we sit down to breakfast. "I hate oatmeal at home," I tell Grandma. "But yours tastes different."

"That's because I am your grandma," she says.

After breakfast Grandma tells me, "It will be windy and bitter cold tonight. We'll need plenty of wood for our stove." We pull on boots and mittens and go outside.

I am taking great high steps through the snow when suddenly I let go of Grandma's hand. I fall backward, and Grandma falls beside me. We wave our arms and legs, shushing them through the snow to make two snow angels, a grandma and a little girl.

We brush each other off. Then we carry wood and stack it in the kitchen.

Later, after we have warmed our hands around mugs of hot cocoa, Grandma sets peanut butter, cornmeal, and pine cones on the table.

"Is this lunch?" I ask.

Grandma laughs. "Not for us," she says. "It's for our friends the birds."

"But Grandma," I say, "last summer we shooed the birds away."

"That's because they were pecking our fruit even though they had food of their own," Grandma answers. "But now their food is covered with snow, and they are cold and hungry."

We mix peanut butter and cornmeal in a bowl and press the mixture into the pine cones. Grandma has saved field corn for the squirrels. I will share an apple with the rabbits.

As we hang up the pine cones for the birds, I wonder how we will find the rabbits. Grandma points to tiny tracks in the snow.

We follow the tracks to a small plum tree we planted last summer. Grandma stops and sighs. "Just as I suspected," she says. "The rabbits are nibbling my promises."

"Promises?" I ask.

Kneeling, Grandma shows me buds growing along the branches. "Inside each is next summer's leaf," she explains. "For me, buds are the promise of summer when you will come again."

Together we sprinkle apple peelings to lead the rabbits away from the tree.

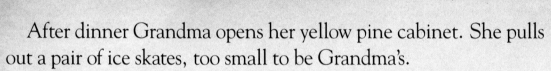

After dinner Grandma opens her yellow pine cabinet. She pulls out a pair of ice skates, too small to be Grandma's.

"Whose skates are those?" I ask.

"They were your mother's when she was a little girl," Grandma says. " Let's see if they fit you." Grandma slips a skate onto my foot. "Why, Kim, they're exactly the right size!"

"These were my mother's?" I say.

"Yes," Grandma answers. "She liked to skate on our pond. Now it's your turn to use them."

I think about skating on the pond in my mother's skates as I listen to the fire rustle and pop inside the wood stove. Soon my sleepy eyes start to close.

"Time for bed," says Grandma. She is holding a stack of blankets. "Tonight will be an adventure. We'll make a bedroll and sleep in front of the wood stove."

Together Grandma and I make a thick layer of blankets on the floor. We make the corners neat and tuck in three sides. I crawl into the bedroll first, and Grandma gets in beside me. Outside, branches creak against the wind. Indoors, I snuggle like a squirrel, safe and warm in Grandma's arms.

In the morning Grandma says it's too windy for skating, but not for a treasure hunt.

We hunt treasures in Grandma's attic. I help Grandma move piles of stiff yellow papers off a big brown trunk. The dust tickles my nose. Inside the trunk I find clothes—sweaters, hats, and my mother's green party dress. We try everything on.

Beside me, Grandma's smile seems to fill the mirror. "Kim, you look just like your mother!"

But when I look I only see me.

The next afternoon, we walk to the pond. I have never skated on a pond before. At first I wobble over bumpy ice, but then I reach a patch licked smooth by the wind. Now I can glide fast and far, but I can always see Grandma.

I like it when Grandma watches me. Later I will ask her, Could my mother skate backwards when she was a little girl like me?

We're on our way home when
suddenly Grandma stops. "Shhh," she
says. I look where she is pointing.
"Santa's reindeer!" I whisper.
"No, Kim," Grandma whispers back.
"Those are white-tailed deer."

Walking slowly, we watch until their white tails disappear among the trees. I am thinking of the white-tailed deer when Grandma squeezes my arm. "Look, Kim! The electricity is on!"

Grandma's windows are glowing with yellow light. "Hooray!" I shout, even though I will miss the adventure of sleeping in front of the wood stove.

A few days later my peephole is gone, and the sun beams through my window. Outside, the snow is softer. I find rabbit tracks, larger than before.

"Grandma, do you have a monster rabbit?" I ask.

Grandma smiles. "No, Kim. The tracks got bigger when the snow melted. Why, just look at yours. They're big enough to be next year's prints."

"Oh, no," I groan. "Then my mother's skates won't fit."

Grandma puts her arms around me.

"We'll buy you skates of your own," she says. "But for now, I think you should take your mother's skates home. They'll help you remember that no matter how big you grow, you can always come back to Grandma's."

"Promise, Grandma?" I ask.
"Promise," Grandma answers.